P9-DXE-986

STONE ARCH BOOKS
a capstone imprint

STONE ARCH BOOKS
Published in 2013
A Capstone Imprint
1710 Roe Crest Drive
North Mankato, MN 56003
www.capstonepub.com

DC Comics
1700 Broadway, New York, NY 10019
A Warner Bros. Entertainment Company

Cataloging-in-Publication Data is available at the Library of
Congress website:
ISBN: 978-1-4342-4697-4 (library binding)

Summary: New pals Blue Beetle and Supergirl stop by the
Tiny Titans' Treehouse! Plus, even more crazy capers!

Ashley C. Andersen Zantop *Publisher*
Michael Dahl *Editorial Director*
Donald Lemke & Alison Deering *Editors*
Heather Kindseth *Creative Director*
Hilary Wacholz *Designer*
Kathy McColley *Production Specialist*

DC COMICS
Jann Jones *Original U.S. Editor*
Stephanie Buscema *U.S. Assistant Editor*

Printed in the United States of America in
North, Mankato, Minnesota.
042017 010473R

tiny titans

Welcome to the Treehouse

By Eisner Winners
Art Baltazar & Franco

tiny titans

ROBIN

STARFIRE

RAVEN

KID FLASH

MISS MARTIAN

KID DEVIL

CASSIE

BEAST BOY

AQUALAD

WONDER GIRL

BUMBLEBEE

CYBORG

ROSE

SPEEDY

5

ROBIN

(Dick Grayson)- The brave and serious leader of the Tiny Titans. Although he is the original Robin, he is very moody and has to share his room with his brothers, the other Robins.
Also, he has secret crushes for Starfire and Barbara Gordon.

JASON TODDLER

The youngest of the three Robins. Too young to go to school, Jason is always in a happy mood and has a care-free style. He's all about smiling and having fun.

TIM DRAKE

The cool Robin. Tim wants to stand out from his brothers by wearing his own unique Robin costume. He's very laid back and easy going indeed.

KID FLASH

The super speedster and fasted kid in the school. Quick witted and eats lots for lunch because of his high metabolism. Too much candy will cause major sugar rush.

AQUALAD

The little boy from the ocean. Has a pet fish named Fluffy. Aqualad can communicate with all forms of sea life, even the pet hamster in their classroom.

SPEEDY

Quiet and cool, he is the boy with the trick arrows. He's good at anything that requires aiming. Also, he's Kid Flash's best friend.

WONDER GIRL

(Donna) Raised by amazons. She's strong and cute. Never lie to her, she has a magical jump rope which makes people tell the truth. Very skeptic.

RAVEN

The quiet and mysterious little girl. She really likes to experiment with dark magic, which usually turn into bad practical jokes. Mr. Trigon, the substitute teacher is her father.

CYBORG

Half boy, half robot. Cyborg is always tinkering with mechanical gadgets, often turning them into something else. His battle cry "BOO-YA!" has earned him the nickname, "Big Boo-Ya".

BEAST BOY

The green little boy who can change into any animal he desires. He's a prankster and loves comics. Has a crush on Terra.

STARFIRE

She's an alien princess. Very naïve and free spirited and finds the good in others. Has a crush on Robin and thinks he's cute, but so do all the other girls.

KID DEVIL

One of the younger Tiny Titans, still too young for school. Cannot talk but can breathe fire, usually while coughing or sneezing or hiccupping.

ROSE & JERICHO

Principal Slade's kids. Rose is the older and tougher "Tom-Boy" of the two. Jericho can't speak, but can take over your mind if you look into his eyes.

MISS MARTIAN

A shape shifting little girl alien from Mars who is still too young to go to school. She is often mistaken for Beast Boy's little sister.

TERRA

The sometimes hated little girl who likes to throw rocks. Principal Slade's teacher's pet. She thinks Beast Boy is a weirdo.

CASSIE

Wonder Girl's rich cousin from the big city. Cassie's really into fashion and is hip to all the latest trends in POP culture.

BUMBLE BEE

The tiniest of the Tiny Titans. BB buzzes and packs a mighty stinger.

Creators

Art Baltazar is a cartoonist machine from the heart of Chicago! He defines cartoons and comics not only as an art style, but as a way of life. Currently, Art is the creative force behind *The New York Times* best-selling, Eisner Award-winning, DC Comics series Tiny Titans, and the co-writer for Billy Batson and the Magic of SHAZAM! and co-creator of Superman Family Adventures. Art is living the dream! He draws comics and never has to leave the house. He lives with his lovely wife, Rose, big boy Sonny, little boy Gordon, and little girl Audrey. Right on!

ART BALTAZAR

FRANCO

Bronx, New York born writer and artist Franco Aureliani has been drawing comics since he could hold a crayon. Currently residing in upstate New York with his wife, Ivette, and son, Nicolas, Franco spends most of his days in a Batcave-like studio where he produces DC's Tiny Titans comics. In 1995, Franco founded Blindwolf Studios, an independent art studio where he and fellow creators can create children's comics. Franco is the creator, artist, and writer of Weirdsville, L'il Creeps, and Eagle All Star, as well as the co-creator and writer of Patrick the Wolf Boy. When he's not writing and drawing, Franco also teaches high school art.

Glossary

ALLOW [uh·LOU] – let someone have or do something

LAGOON [luh·GOON] – a shallow pool of seawater seperated from the sea by a narrow strip of land

MADAM [MAD·uhm] – a formal title for a woman

OUTFIT [OUT·fit] – a set of clothes

PARDON [PARD·uhn] – to forgive or excuse someone

SHY [SHYE] – bashful or not comfortable around people or with strangers

SUBBING [SUHB·ing] – serving in the place of another, such as a substitute teacher

Action Accessories

Speedy

BOW AND ARROW

Robin

CAPE

Terra

ROCKS

Aqualad

FLUFFY

Wonder Girl

MAGIC JUMP ROPE

Visual Questions & Prompts

1. WHAT ACTIVITY ARE THE TINY TITANS DOING ON THEIR CAMPING TRIP IN THE PANEL BELOW? IMAGINE SOME OTHER ACTIVITIES THEY MIGHT DO.

2. HOW DOES RAVEN SOLVE THE PET CLUB PROBLEM IN THE PANELS BELOW? THINK ABOUT ANOTHER SOLUTION THE TINY TITANS COULD HAVE USED.

3. IN COMICS, A CHARACTER'S FACIAL EXPRESSIONS OFTEN SHOW YOU WHAT THEY'RE FEELING. HOW DO YOU THINK RAVEN IS FEELING IN THE PANEL AT RIGHT? USE THE ILLUSTRATION TO EXPLAIN YOUR ANSWER.

tiny titans